D0615933

Oswald's Garden

adapted by Heather Feldman
based on the teleplay, "The Tomato Garden," written by Alana San
illustrated by Barry Goldberg

Ready-to-Read

Simon Spotlight/Nick Jr.
New York   London   Toronto   Sydney

Based on the TV series *Oswald*™ as seen on Nick Jr.®

SIMON SPOTLIGHT
An imprint of Simon & Schuster Children's Publishing Division
1230 Avenue of the Americas
New York, New York 10020
Copyright © 2004 HIT Entertainment and Viacom International Inc.
All rights reserved. NICKELODEON, NICK JR.,
Oswald, and all related titles, logos, and characters are trademarks of
Viacom International Inc.

READY-TO-READ, SIMON SPOTLIGHT, and colophon are
registered trademarks of Simon & Schuster, Inc.

Manufactured in the United States of America

First Edition

2 4 6 8 10 9 7 5 3 1

Library of Congress Cataloging-in-Publication Data

Feldman, Heather.
Oswald's garden / adapted by Heather Feldman ; based on the teleplay,
"The tomato garden," written by Alana San.—1st ed.
p. cm.—(Ready-to-read)
"Based on the TV series Oswald as seen on Nick Jr."
Summary: Oswald the blue octopus and his pet, Weenie, plant a tomato
garden, but someone keeps eating their tomatoes.
ISBN 0-689-86836-7
[1. Octopuses—Fiction. 2. Snails—Fiction. 3. Tomatoes—Fiction.]
I. Oswald (Television program) II. Title. III. Series.
PZ7.F335775 Os 2004
[E]—dc22
2003017834

OSWALD and WEENIE

love to eat TOMATOES.

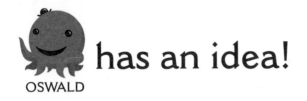

OSWALD **has an idea!**

"We could plant our own garden," says .

TOMATO

OSWALD

They go to the STORE

to buy a 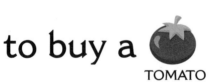  .
TOMATO PLANT

 digs a .
WEENIE   HOLE

 puts the in
OSWALD   PLANT

the .
     HOLE

They water the .
                TOMATO PLANT

They wait . . .

and wait . . .

and wait.

The next day they

see a big  !

TOMATO

"Look!" cries  .

OSWALD

"We need to buy one more .

PLANT

Then we will have

one  for us and one
PLANT

for the !"
SNAILS

They put the new 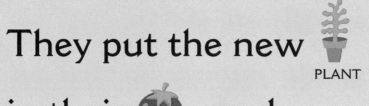 PLANT

in their  TOMATO garden.

The next day they see two big  !

TOMATOES

What will  do?

OSWALD

"I have an idea!"

says .
OSWALD

"Come on, 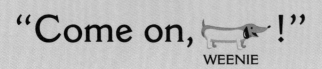!"
WEENIE

OSWALD and WEENIE get to work.

 hammers .

OSWALD BOARDS

 helps paint.

WEENIE

TODAY'S
SPECIAL

"We are open for lunch!"

says  .

OSWALD